RIES

A New Beginning

A New Beginning

Scholastic Inc.

All rights reserved. Published by Scholastic Inc., *Publishers since 1920*. SCHOLASTIC and associated logos are trademarks and/or registered trademarks of Scholastic Inc.

The publisher does not have any control over and does not assume any responsibility for author or third-party websites or their content.

This book is a work of fiction. Names, characters, places, and incidents are either the product of the author's imagination or are used fictitiously, and any resemblance to actual persons, living or dead, business establishments, events, or locales is entirely coincidental.

ISBN 978-1-338-67084-4

10 9 8 7 6 5 4 3 2 1   20 21 22 23 24

Printed in the U.S.A.   40

First printing 2020

Book design by Cheung Tai

Contents

Chapter 1

Pallet Town, in the Kanto region, when Ash Ketchum was still too young to be a Pokémon Trainer...

Hey, Mom!" Ash yelled, racing into the kitchen. He was waving a flyer covered with pictures of Pokémon. "Can I go to Professor Oak's Pokémon Camp?!" He wanted to learn as much about Pokémon as he could, and Professor Oak was an expert!

"Oh, so they have a camp for that, too! All right, I'll fill out your application," his mom replied.

"Yay!" Ash cheered, leaping around the kitchen.

"But I have an early appointment that day that I can't change," his mom continued. "Are you sure you can wake yourself up?"

Ash was so excited about camp and the Pokémon he would see there that he was barely listening to his mom. "It'll be so much fun!" he cried.

Meanwhile, in the forest outside Pallet Town, an enthusiastic Pichu was running through the trees. In the wilderness, there were many Pokémon who live in groups, but this little Electric-type Pokémon seemed to be all alone.

The Pichu was playing happily when an Ekans slithered out, hissing, and charged at it. Startled, Pichu used Thunder Shock on the Ekans—which jolted it so powerfully that the Snake Pokémon thumped to the ground and slithered away in fear!

Pichu thumped to the ground in a daze, too. It was still learning how to control its electricity, and it was exhausted from the attack.

After it recovered, the Tiny Mouse Pokémon kept wandering through the forest. It saw many different groups of Pokémon living together, from Mankey to Nidoran to Dodrio. But there were no other Pichu.

As Pichu stood at an overlook, feeling lonely, three

Koffing floated by. Suddenly, thèy used Smokescreen, filling the air around the little Pokémon with thick green smoke. It made Pichu gasp and cough—and accidentally tumble off the cliff!

"*Piiichuuuuuu!*" it cried as it fell down, down, down . . . until it landed safely in the paws of a Kangaskhan.

The Kangaskhan was so big that Pichu was scared. It tried to scurry away. Then it realized the Parent Pokémon meant it no harm—and there was a baby Kangaskhan in its pouch who was almost as small as Pichu!

Kangaskhan gently lowered Pichu to the ground, and the little Kangaskhan jumped down, too.

"*Kanga!*" it chirped in greeting.

"*Pi, pichu!*" Pichu replied.

They were friends in no time!

Pichu looked around the clearing and saw that it was full of Kangaskhan with babies in their pouches. Soon, one Kangaskhan called out to the group. It was time for them to leave that area of the forest.

As the other Pokémon started to walk away, Pichu felt very disappointed. It wanted to play more with the

little Kangaskhan, but instead, it was going to be alone in the forest again.

Luckily, the Kangaskhan who had caught the Tiny Mouse Pokémon looked back and saw it looking sad. It came over, picked Pichu up—and put it right into its pouch, next to its own baby!

"Pichu, pi pichu!" Pichu cheered. It chattered away to its new best friend.

The group made its way to a cluster of Oran trees. The grown-up Kangaskhan plucked two Oran

Berries and gave one to its baby Kangaskhan, who gulped it right down, and one to Pichu. But Pichu wasn't sure what to do with it. It offered the Berry to its friend, but the big Kangaskhan grabbed it before the little one could eat it. That Berry was for Pichu! The Kangaskhan demonstrated opening its mouth wide, then popped the Oran Berry into Pichu's mouth.

   "Pi pichuuu!" How delicious!

The Kangaskhan had truly taken Pichu in, and Pichu was lonely no longer! It was happy to stay with its new Pokémon pals.

Chapter 2

A few weeks later . . .

It was the first day of Professor Oak's Pokémon Camp. A group of kids faced the professor outside his lab near the forest, waiting for camp to start.

"Uh, Professor, isn't it time to be on our way?" a young girl named Chloe asked. She was ready to explore.

"Yes, but I'm afraid we're missing somebody," Professor Oak answered. "We're waiting on a lively young man who lives in the neighborhood." He was talking about Ash!

A young boy named Goh piped up. "I know what! I bet he was so excited about our trip, he couldn't sleep!"

"You might have a point there," Professor Oak said. "Wait, what was your name?"

Goh pointed to Chloe. "She invited me along. I'm Goh!"

"He comes to watch the research at my dad's lab all the time," Chloe said.

Professor Oak knew Chloe's dad. His name was Professor Cerise. "Chloe's father does lots of research on Pokémon, just like me," Professor Oak explained to the group.

After a few more minutes, he decided they'd waited for Ash long enough. The Pokémon Camp began without him as the group made their way into the forest.

Just then, Ash bolted up in bed.

"Oh no! What time is it?" he cried. He'd thrown his alarm clock against the wall while he was dreaming, and ended up oversleeping!

Ash got ready as quickly as he could and sprinted out the door . . . but it was too late. Ash would have to

wait for another day to learn about Pokémon from Professor Oak.

Back in the forest, Professor Oak was leading the young campers through the trees. They came upon a Trainer whose Squirtle was battling a Caterpie.

"Whoa! A wild Caterpie!" Goh cried. They all watched as the Trainer threw her Poké Ball and caught the Pokémon. The campers were very impressed.

"When you turn ten, *you* can become Trainers!" Professor Oak told them. "But before then, you'll want to learn everything you can about Pokémon!"

The kids all cheered in agreement, except for Goh. "There probably isn't a thing about Pokémon I don't know," he said confidently.

"*Goh*...," Chloe muttered. Her friend's bragging embarrassed her.

Professor Oak chuckled. "Sounds like you're quite the expert!" he said. They continued walking through the forest, and then he pointed at a Pokémon just off the path. "Now, who can tell me something about this Pokémon?"

Goh answered right away. "It's the Cocoon Pokémon, Kakuna!"

"Ooh, precisely!" Professor Oak said. As another Pokémon crossed in front of them, he said, "Then you probably know this one, too."

"That's a Farfetch'd!" Goh exclaimed. "It's got a plant stalk that it can swing like a sword and slice up all kinds of stuff!"

The other kids at the camp were very impressed.

"Wow!" one said.

"You *do* know everything!" said another.

Goh leaped forward and pointed at a Pokémon he saw sticking out of the ground. "That's a Diglett! It likes to eat tree roots!" he cried. Then he saw another Pokémon and pointed at it eagerly. "The evolved form of Diglett, Dugtrio! They've got amazing power—they can dig tunnels at over sixty miles per hour!"

"'Scuse me," Chloe said. "We *do* have Professor Oak here to give us the facts on Pokémon..." She wished Goh wouldn't act like such a know-it-all!

Professor Oak laughed. "I have to admit, Goh is

quite knowledgeable!" he said. Then he started telling the group about Pokémon Evolution. "All right. As Goh previously mentioned, Pokémon evolve. Conditions for Evolution vary among Pokémon, but–"

Goh interrupted him. "That Farfetch'd doesn't evolve, right?"

Professor Oak was startled but admitted Goh was correct.

"It's not like every Pokémon on the planet evolves," Goh continued. "The fact is, there are some Pokémon who actually don't!"

"'Scuse me . . . ," said Chloe, who was embarrassed again.

Professor Oak didn't seem to mind Goh's disrespect, but Chloe pulled him aside. "Honestly, Goh!" she said. "This is exactly why you never make friends!"

"Who said I wanted to make friends, anyway?" Goh replied. "What I want is to catch a Pokémon that nobody has ever seen before!"

Chloe looked doubtful, which annoyed Goh. "Don't make fun of me!" he said.

"You're talking like you're in a dream," Chloe answered.

"It's reality!" Goh insisted. "It's my future! And I can hold that future in the palm of my hand!"

Chloe was still skeptical. But before she could say anything, they were interrupted by a roar in the distance.

"*Nidooo!*"

"It's a Nidoking!" Goh cried. They could see the large purple Drill Pokémon battling another Pokémon—but which Pokémon was it? Goh could

see that the other Pokémon was small and light pink, and it twirled through the air with a playful giggle.

Just as Nidoking's Earth Power move was about to strike it, the other Pokémon suddenly disappeared in midair—and then reappeared on the other side of Nidoking!

"You're kidding!" Goh shrieked.

But he was about to be even more amazed. The other Pokémon playfully attacked Nidoking—using Nidoking's own Earth Power move!

"*Mew! Mew!*" the Pokémon said, giggling and spinning in the air as Nidoking recovered.

Nidoking was angry. It threw a huge Sludge Wave at its opponent.

The small pink Pokémon disappeared and re-appeared elsewhere, dodging the attack, and then threw Sludge Wave right back at Nidoking.

"It used the same move again!" Goh said. He couldn't tear his eyes off the battle.

Nidoking was getting frustrated. It launched a Fire Blast, but the other Pokémon once again dodged the attack by disappearing and reappearing. Then it sent a Fire Blast back to Nidoking, knocking it out.

Goh was mesmerized. "Who's that Pokémon?" he asked.

"*Mew?*" The Pokémon noticed Goh and Chloe, and then sped away through the air. Goh sprinted after it, with Chloe close behind.

"Goh, wait up!" she called.

They ran and ran. Goh thought he'd lost the Pokémon. Then a Magmar appeared. But it actually wasn't Magmar at all . . . it soon transformed into the playful pink Pokémon!

Goh realized this was the most powerful and fascinating Pokémon he'd ever seen. He and Chloe kept chasing it. As it ran ahead, it transformed again, this time into Tauros. It charged forward, approaching the river. Then it leaped into the air, transformed back into itself—and then transformed into Lapras before landing in the water!

"It won't get away from *me*!" Goh cried.

Farther ahead in the forest was a certain Pichu who had become great friends with a group of Kangaskhan. While some Chansey came by to share some eggs with the Kangaskhan, Pichu's little Kangaskhan pal was exploring the riverbank nearby.

A Lapras swam by it—and then transformed into the small pink Pokémon! The little Kangaskhan was transfixed. The pink Pokémon flew over to it, then played hide-and-seek with it by disappearing and reappearing again. They were both having a great time!

When the pink Pokémon started flying away, high up into the air, the little Kangaskhan followed it, climbing higher and higher up the rocks by the river.

Meanwhile, it was time for the group of Kangaskhan to eat their Chansey eggs, but one Kangaskhan could not find its baby. Its pal Pichu was there to eat, but the little Kangaskhan was nowhere to be seen!

Pichu and Kangaskhan looked and looked for the little Kangaskhan. Finally, they saw it—way up on top of a cliff.

"*Kangaskhaaaan!*" the Parent Pokémon called.

By this point, Goh and Chloe were just across the river, where they'd been trying to catch up to the mysterious pink Pokémon.

While the little Kangaskhan was chasing its new playmate, it stepped too close to the edge of the cliff. Suddenly, the rock it was standing on crumbled away, and the little Pokémon fell down, down, down . . .

Goh and Chloe saw it falling, but there was nothing they could do. They were too far away.

The pink Pokémon also saw what had happened, and it acted quickly. It used its powers to stop the little Kangaskhan in midair! Then it floated the little Kangaskhan gently down into the arms of its

parent, safe and sound. The mysterious pink Pokémon zipped away across the sky. It had saved the day!

As Goh and Chloe were watching it fly off, Professor Oak came running up.

"So this is where you two have been!" he said, panting. "I looked all over!"

They told him about the pink Pokémon they'd been chasing, and asked what kind of Pokémon it might be.

"Hmmm . . . I'm not certain, but it could be Mew," he said.

"Mew?" Goh asked. He wanted to know everything about it.

"They say it lives in the depths of the jungle, but it's said to be able to vanish at will, so it hasn't been seen by many people," the professor explained. "It's believed to be a Mythical Pokémon whose DNA resembles the DNA of all other Pokémon."

Chloe was interested. "An extremely rare Pokémon?"

"Awesome!" Goh cheered. This was exactly the Pokémon he had been dreaming of! "Man, I wanna be ten years old now so I can become a Pokémon Trainer! Then I'll be able to catch Mew, the ultra-awesome Pokémon!"

Chapter 3

Time passed, and both Pichu and the little Kangaskhan grew a little bit bigger. It was becoming harder for the big Kangaskhan to carry both Pokémon, though it wasn't ready to let them go. When Pichu tried to walk on its own to help lighten the load, Kangaskhan picked it right back up and put it in its pouch.

But Pichu knew it was almost time to leave and strike out on its own again. It couldn't stay with these Kangaskhan forever.

One night, while the group was asleep in a cave, Pichu hopped out of the Kangaskhan's pouch. Kangaskhan and its baby kept sleeping peacefully, and Pichu made its way out into the moonlight.

"*Pi-chu*," it said, looking back at the cave sadly.

Pichu had been so happy with the group of Kangaskhan, who had welcomed it as one of their own. The Tiny Mouse Pokémon thought back fondly on all it had shared with those Pokémon, from first meeting them and learning to eat Oran Berries to playing with the little Kangaskhan every day.

The full moon glowed in the sky as a tear dripped down Pichu's face.

Suddenly, Pichu was enveloped in a blast of light brighter than the moon. It was evolving! A moment later . . .

"*Pika?*" It was now a Pikachu!

Pikachu looked at its reflection in a puddle, then leaped around in delight, admiring its new lightning-bolt-shaped tail. "*Pika! Pikachuuu!*"

It waved good-bye to its friends in the cave and

then scampered off into the forest to begin its first day as a Pikachu.

Good-byes may not be easy, but they can lead to brand-new, happy hellos...

Some time later, Ash Ketchum had just celebrated his tenth birthday. On the day when he was to begin his journey as a Pokémon Trainer, Ash threw his alarm clock against the wall while he was dreaming, and overslept—again! But this time, he didn't completely miss out.

He sprinted to Professor Oak's lab and was given his first partner Pokémon. A flash of light revealed a very special Pikachu who had been living in the forest nearby. It was once a lonely Pichu, and now . . .

"Hi, Pikachu!" Ash said as he started to hug it. "You and I are gonna be best friends!"

Pikachu, of course, immediately jolted Ash with Thunder Shock.

"It usually avoids contact with humans," Professor Oak said. "Use caution, or you'll be shocked."

Ash soon recovered, dazed but excited. "So you're Pikachu!" he said. "My name's Ash! Nice to meet you!"

And so, from that moment, Ash and Pikachu's story began. Since then, they've had many adventures together—and they're always ready for the next one!

Chapter 4

Pallet Town, present day ...

Ash's alarm clock beeped and beeped, though he and Pikachu remained sound asleep. In his sleep, Ash grabbed the clock and threw it across the room—which woke up Pikachu but not Ash. Was he about to oversleep *again*?

Even Pikachu's Thunderbolt move didn't wake Ash—but luckily, Ash's mom, Delia, came into his room.

"Are you still asleep?" she asked. "You'll be late getting to Professor Oak's lab!"

Finally, Ash woke up. He scrambled around to get out of the house as quickly as he could, and then sprinted to the lab with Pikachu close behind.

"Professor Oak!" he called. "What did you want to talk to me about?"

The professor explained, "Actually, a protégé of mine has just opened a brand-new research facility in Vermilion City. I was hoping to invite you to the opening ceremony. You will come, won't you?"

"Sure!" Ash was excited. He turned to Pikachu and said, "You'll come, too, right?"

But just then, Ash's mom walked up to the lab with Mimey, her Mr. Mime Pokémon partner. She thought Ash had been talking to her. "I'd love to!" she responded.

"I came to deliver your lunch, but what a great idea—all those delicious sweet shops and big fashion boutiques in Vermilion City!"

That was a surprise! Ash wasn't thrilled that his mom would be joining his trip with Professor Oak, but what could he do? At least he knew his mom would be doing her own thing once they got to the city.

On their drive to Vermilion City, Ash watched the countryside go by. He was daydreaming about becoming a Pokémon Master. Who knew what Pokémon he might meet on his visit?

Once they arrived, Delia and Mimey got out to go

shopping, and Professor Oak dropped off Ash at the steps of the research facility.

"I'll park the car. You go on ahead," he said.

"Right!" Ash said, bounding out of the car with Pikachu.

As they made their way up the long flight of stairs, a small "brown-yellow-and-white" Pokémon approached them. Ash was immediately interested.

"Wow! A Pokémon I've never seen before!" Ash cried. He crept forward on the stairs, trying to reach the little Pokémon. "You're such a cutie! What's your name?" he asked. "Let me pet you just a little!"

But the Pokémon growled and backed up. "*Yamp, yamp!*" it said angrily, hopping around to avoid Ash's grasp.

Finally, Ash put on a burst of speed and grabbed it, giving it a big hug. "Got ya now . . . ," he said. Pikachu was embarrassed about Ash's behavior—but it knew it couldn't stop him.

"*Yamp! Yamp!*" The Pokémon had had enough. It hit Ash with Spark.

Ash screamed as he was electrified—he didn't know this Pokémon was an Electric-type!

While Ash recovered on the ground, the Puppy Pokémon came over and made friends with Pikachu,

licking it on the cheek. They bounded in a circle, playing. Just then, Chloe walked up the stairs, on her way home from school.

"Hello, Yamper, I'm home—" Chloe gasped, noticing Ash on the ground and tiptoed around him. Her Electric-type Pokémon pal, Yamper, followed close behind.

Soon Professor Oak found Ash, too. "If you don't get a move on, you'll miss the opening ceremony!" he said.

That got Ash up! He shook off his shock and hurried inside the grand building. The ceremony was taking place in a large stone hall that was already full of other people. Ash strained to see around them to the stage at the end of the hall.

A man with brown hair and glasses came onto the stage and introduced himself.

"Thank you for coming. I am Professor Cerise, owner of the Cerise Research Laboratory. Now, let's move on to the subject of Pokémon." He snapped his fingers, and a high-tech computer shot up beams of light that formed a digital screen. It projected pictures of Pokémon as he continued to speak.

"As you're already aware, our planet plays host to this mysterious life-form. In forests, in the sky, and under the seas, no matter where you go in this world, you will undoubtedly find them," he said. Ash knew this was true. From Kakuna and Butterfree in the woods, to Pidgeot in the sky, to Horsea

and Tentacruel in the water, there were Pokémon everywhere!

Professor Cerise continued. "And so, as Pokémon and humans live together in our world, they bond with each other in many ways. We at the Cerise Laboratory are dedicated to uncovering the mysteries of Pokémon in every region ... investigating, analyzing, digging deep, and expanding our knowledge. Because to know Pokémon is to know the world! And that is the very key to making it a *better* world for each and every one of us!"

Ash was riveted. This was a lab with a great mission!

Chapter 5

Upstairs, in the living quarters above the great stone hall, Chloe was reading on the couch. She looked affectionately at Yamper dozing beside her, then sighed and put her book down. As she walked over to look out the window, Yamper woke up and scampered over to her side.

"Come on, Goh," Chloe said as she gazed outside, looking for her friend. "You told me you'd be stopping by today, and that's why I brought your homework here with me."

Just then, her phone pinged. It was a text message from Goh, and she read it aloud, annoyed. "'I'm going to be late because I'm about to have a fateful encounter'?!" Chloe huffed in frustration. "Wow . . . the only time he gets in touch is for nonsense like this!"

Meanwhile, Goh was across town, high up on the roof of a big building on a hill. He was surrounded by books, and he held up his phone as it performed complicated calculations.

"Just as I predicted!" Goh exclaimed. "These are the exact cloud formations needed for its arrival! This'll be a breeze!"

At the same time, in the great stone hall at the lab, Professor Cerise's phone beeped with an alert. He looked at it with a furrowed brow. "Let's see . . ." He opened up a new screen on the high-tech computer he was displaying on the stage. "The atmospheric circulation, temperature, humidity, altitude . . . This may not be the most accurate forecast, but in about twenty minutes, an extremely rare Pokémon might just appear over Vermilion Port."

"A rare Pokémon?" Ash was thrilled to hear that!

Professor Cerise showed Professor Oak his phone, and Professor Oak agreed that it seemed likely.

Ash shot his hand up to interrupt. "Professors?! I'll go and check it out, 'kay?"

"Pi, pikachu!" Pikachu called from Ash's shoulder as they dashed out the door.

Everyone else in the crowd started murmuring excitedly, making guesses about what the rare Pokémon could be.

Ash ran through the city, happy that every street he passed was empty. He wanted to beat everyone to the rare Pokémon!

"Okay, I'm the first one!" he cheered. He was feeling great about himself. He was sure that he'd get to battle the rare Pokémon before anyone else.

Suddenly, Pikachu squealed in alarm. *"Pika! Pi, pikaaa!"*

But it was too late—Ash slammed right into a Snorlax asleep in the middle of the street!

He and Pikachu bounced backward, spitting out Snorlax fur. Gross!

"Snorlax?! Give me a break! Move over!" Ash

pleaded. It was completely blocking the way forward. *Now* how would they get to the rare Pokémon?

While Ash was figuring out how to get past the Sleeping Pokémon, Goh was still on top of the building, ready to be the first to see the rare Pokémon. According to his calculations, it would be appearing in just a moment!

"Here it comes," he said. "Five . . . four . . . three . . . two . . . one . . . Go!"

But nothing happened.

"That's weird . . . ," Goh said.

Suddenly, he heard a Pokémon nearby—but it was just a Psyduck passing by behind him. *"Psyyyyy . . . ,"* it said, holding its head in its hands.

Goh was frustrated. "What's with you?!" he demanded.

Then a big flash of lightning called Goh's attention back to the sky. An enormous black thundercloud was swirling in the distance! But the cloud was not right above Goh, as he'd thought it would be. It was over a totally different part of the city, by the port.

He had to get over there. But would he make it in time?

The people who happened to already be over by the port were riveted by the huge, swirling cloud and flashing lightning. A smaller ball of clouds appeared within it, and soon beams of light started to shoot out from its center. The ball burst open, revealing . . . Lugia!

The Legendary Pokémon flapped its huge white wings and let out a cry.

Three Pokémon Trainers nearby were immediately ready to battle Lugia. They each threw down a Poké Ball, and then commanded their Pokémon:

"Wartortle! Use Ice Beam!"

"Jolteon, Thunder!"

"Gengar, use Night Shade!"

Each Pokémon threw their best moves at Lugia, but the attacks didn't seem to affect it. Instead, Lugia blasted them back with Gust—a wind so powerful, it blew all three Pokémon straight back into their Trainers' arms!

Lugia swooped over to a different area along the water's edge, where a different group of five Trainers was eager to battle it.

"Let's all do this together!" said a man with glasses.

"Yeah, a raid battle!" agreed another Trainer.

They all tossed their Poké Balls and called out moves to their Pokémon. Sableye, Sudowoodo, and Bisharp charged forward and made their attacks. Garchomp and Corviknight even flew up to the huge Legendary Pokémon. But Lugia easily swiped them back with its wings, knocking all five Pokémon out of the way at once with a powerful Aeroblast.

A moment later, Ash finally made it to the port— and found himself face-to-face with Lugia! Yes!

"There you are!" he called. "Lugia, let's have a battle!"

"*Piiika pi!*" Pikachu was ready.

Lugia nodded its assent, and the battle began.

"Pikachu, use Thunderbolt, now!" Ash said.

"*Piii . . . kaa . . . chuuuuu!*" Pikachu gathered up its energy and hit Lugia with a Thunderbolt. But again, the attack didn't seem to bother Lugia, who shot a huge Aeroblast back, making Pikachu tumble back- ward through the air. Ash slid forward and caught Pikachu just before it hit the ground. They were outmatched.

Lugia started to fly away.

"Hey, wait!" Ash called. He ran after it up the moun- tain road as fast as he could.

Chapter 6

*G*oh was running toward Lugia, too—from the other direction.

"The future's in the palm of my hand!" he said, pumping himself up as he got closer and closer.

Goh and Ash were each determined to get to Lugia in any way possible. At the same moment, they both launched themselves off different parts of the city's steepest mountain road—and *onto* Lugia!

Goh landed on its tail, and Ash landed on its leg. Both were hanging on to the Legendary Pokémon with all their strength, trying to make their way up to its back as it soared through the air.

They noticed each other at the same time. "What are you doing here?!" they both screamed. Neither of them had been expecting to encounter someone else doing the same crazy thing!

Lugia spun around in a corkscrew, and both boys yelled in panic as they tried not to fall off.

Finally, Ash made it up to the Legendary Pokémon's back, and helped pull Goh up, too. They both sat there catching their breath for a moment, and Lugia looked back with a friendly expression.

"Whoa, Lugia . . . ," Ash said. It was starting to sink in that they were truly up on top of the Diving Pokémon!

Goh came to the same realization. "Awesome! I'm riding on top of Lugia right now!" he said, amazed. He observed the way the Legendary Pokémon flew, and held up his phone to start recording his experience. "So that's how its back fins move . . . wow!"

He rubbed his hand on Lugia's shimmery back. "It's a lot rougher than I thought," he said, still recording.

"Check it out!" Ash called. He was hugging one of Lugia's back fins and bobbing up and down along with it. "It feels so warm!"

Just then, Lugia let out a deafening roar. Ash and Goh covered their ears and crouched down. The Pokémon shot up, up, up in the air! Lugia's passengers screamed and held on for dear life until it finally leveled out, high in the sky. They were coasting right by a group of Pokémon that were flying.

"Fearow!" Ash said with a happy laugh. He held out his hand to try to touch one, while Goh recorded with his phone.

"For them to be just as high as Lugia, they must have amazing flying power!" Goh said, impressed. It was so cool to see in person how these Pokémon interacted.

Lugia flew at the head of a big V of Fearow. Ash and Goh relaxed and admired the view . . . until Lugia started diving straight down toward the water!

"Aaaaahhhh!" Ash and Goh screamed, bracing for impact.

"*Pika, pikaaaa!*" Pikachu was terrified, too!

Right before they smashed into the water, Lugia used Hydro Pump. That sent a big blast of air into the water, making it splash aside and creating a deep cavern. A beautiful rainbow arched overhead. Ash and Goh were in awe. It felt like they were diving down next to a waterfall as Lugia swooped into the cavern it had created.

Just in time, Ash noticed Lugia was about to break through the water wall and take them all underwater. He, Pikachu, and Goh held their breath as they clung to Lugia's back. After a moment, they were underwater, and they all opened their eyes to take in the amazing Pokémon around them. They passed so many—Shellder, Cloyster, Krabby . . . Tentacruel, Magikarp, Starmie . . . a group of Dewgong, and many more!

Goh started filming. He even said, "Whoa!" aloud before he remembered he was underwater when several Horsea and a Seadra drifted close to him!

The playful Horsea flitted over to Ash and Pikachu. *"Seaaa seaaa!"*

Soon, though, Ash, Pikachu, and Goh started to run out of air. Luckily, Lugia was already headed toward the surface. It burst back into the air in a swirl of water.

As Lugia's massive wings took its passengers higher in the sky, they breathed in deep and sighed with relief.

"That was close . . . ," Goh gasped.

"You know what?" Ash said. "It was awesome to meet so many Pokémon!"

Goh was surprised at Ash's reaction, and then he laughed. "You're pretty funny, you know!" he said.

"Yeah? You think so?" Ash replied.

"Yup! I've decided: You're going to be my friend," Goh said. "I'm Goh, from Vermilion City."

"I'm Ash, from Pallet Town," Ash replied. "This is my partner, Pikachu."

"*Pika-chuuu!*" Pikachu introduced itself as well, jumping onto Ash's shoulder.

Ash and Goh shook hands. "Nice to meet you!" they both said.

Goh reached out to touch Pikachu and got a little electric jolt.

"Pika!" Pikachu said playfully, and they all laughed.

Lugia had been flying quickly, and it suddenly dove downward again. This time, it leveled out just above a meadow where two Rapidash were galloping, their flaming manes flickering behind them.

Lugia's passengers were just waving good-bye to the Rapidash when Lugia took a sharp turn upward. Ash, Goh, and Pikachu all tumbled off its back!

They hurtled downward . . . but a Vileplume in the

meadow broke their fall. One by one, they bounced off it into the grass. When they looked up, there was Lugia hovering above them. It flapped its giant wings in farewell, causing a huge gust of wind that swirled with petals from the flowers in the meadow. The friends braced themselves in the wind, and then waved good-bye as the Legendary Pokémon flew away.

"See you!" Goh said.

"Thanks a lot! Take care!" Ash called.

"Pika, piiikaaa!"

That had been an incredible encounter! They sat quietly in the meadow, reflecting on their amazing experience with Lugia.

"And there it goes . . . ," Goh said with a happy sigh. Some Butterfree fluttered past in the gentle breeze.

"Pokémon are the coolest, huh?" Ash replied, flopping backward onto the grass.

"Yeah. Lugia really brought that feeling home for me—the feeling that there's a lot of world out there!" Goh said, inspired. "You know what? You can go wherever you want, if you've got the desire. And you can meet any Pokémon you want, too!"

Ash sat up energetically. "Yeah, you sure can! No doubt about it!"

"*Pika, pikaaa!*" Pikachu agreed.

They all laughed. What an afternoon it had been!

Goh stood up. "Come on, Ash," he said. "I think it's time we got back."

Ash leaped up, too, worried. "But that's the problem—which way is back?!" They were in the middle of a field, far from town. Lugia hadn't exactly given them precise directions back to the city when it dropped them off!

"*Piiika, piiika . . .*" Pikachu was exasperated.

After a long, long walk, the friends figured out their way and made it back to Vermilion City. They dragged themselves up the steps to Cerise Laboratory and collapsed in front of the door just as the sun was setting.

"Finally . . . we're home . . . ," Ash croaked. They were exhausted.

Yamper came bounding out of the building, yapping away. Pikachu went over to greet it, happy to see its friend again, and Yamper nuzzled Pikachu's cheek.

Chloe came out to see who it was.

"Come on, you're late!" she said to Goh.

"You're not gonna believe what happened—it's the story of our fateful encounter!" Goh said excitedly, looking up at Chloe. "You'll never guess! *I* met Lugia!"

Chloe was not impressed. "Is that so?" she said with a sigh. "This is more important." She handed him a stack of paper. "Here, your homework printouts."

"Right . . . Not that I asked for them in the first place," Goh muttered.

"*Huh?!*" Chloe was annoyed. She'd put effort into

getting Goh's homework for him, and he didn't even seem to care about it!

Goh quickly changed the subject. "That reminds me, where's Professor Cerise?"

"Oh, Dad's inside with Professor Oak," Chloe said.

"What? You mean Professor Oak's here as well?!" Goh exclaimed. He hadn't been at the lab when Ash and the professor had arrived, but he remembered Professor Oak from Pokémon Camp when he was much younger. Goh sprinted inside to say hello.

Ash looked up at Chloe. She was Professor Cerise's daughter? That was interesting!

But before they could talk about it . . . "*Yamp, yamp, yamp!*" Yamper startled Ash by yapping right by his face. That Puppy Pokémon was full of energy!

Chapter 7

Inside the lab, Professor Cerise uploaded the photos and videos from Goh's phone onto his big computer display. He was excited about what Goh had captured!

"I've never seen such close-ups before," he said. "Lugia's back fins while in flight, and clear as day!"

"You haven't seen anything yet!" Goh bragged.

The video continued, and Professor Cerise was even more impressed. "Wait . . . Is this underwater?! This is incredible!" he said.

Goh chuckled with pride.

Professor Oak turned to Ash. "How was *your* experience, Ash?" he asked.

Ash was happy to answer. "You know, for a little while, we actually became friends with Lugia!" he said.

"*Pikachuuu!*" Pikachu confirmed.

But Goh was surprised that Ash described the experience that way. "Became friends?" he asked.

"Where did you get the impression that you were friends?" Professor Cerise added.

Ash turned back to Professor Cerise to explain. "When my eyes met Lugia's, I got this chill!" he said.

"What do you mean by *chill*?" Goh asked, doubtful. "It's just your imagination."

"No, you're wrong about that!" Ash countered. "It's like . . . I'm not sure how to say it . . . It's like when you get those shocks and shivers straight down your spine!"

Goh was starting to understand what Ash meant. "Well, there was that time when Lugia let out a huge Hydro Pump to slow down our descent before hitting the water," he said.

"That's it!" Ash cried. He imagined the moment again—swooping down into the canyon in the sea created by Lugia. "Then, just before we hit the water, I heard a voice saying, 'Here we go!'"

"Heard a voice?!" Goh cried. *He* hadn't heard one!

Professor Cerise was interested. "Ash, that's amazing!" he said, gripping Ash's shoulders.

Ash was a bit taken aback. "Uh, it is?" he said.

"All right, let me say this," said Professor Cerise. "I thank you from the bottom of my heart for what you've done. It's because of you two that I've learned things about Lugia no one's ever known!"

Ash and Goh laughed, honored by the professor's praise. Then Professor Cerise continued. "And so, I have a request," he said. "Will you do me the honor of becoming research fellows at my laboratory?"

"What's a research fellow?" Ash asked.

"It's a special research position, of course!" Goh replied.

"You'll get to meet the many kinds of Pokémon in this world," Professor Cerise explained. "Sharing ideas, communicating, and so much more. You'll be deepening our understanding of Pokémon—all of us, as a team!" He gestured toward the other researchers at the lab.

"I've been waiting to hear those words," Goh said, satisfied. "It's reality! It's my future, and I can hold it in the palm of my hand!"

Just as Goh was really feeling inspired, Ash jumped in front of him, knocking him aside.

"Professor Cerise! I'll do it!" Ash cried. Goh gave him an annoyed look.

"Great!" Professor Cerise said. "Then you'll both agree to my proposal?"

"Yeah, but I'll help you out more than Ash will!" Goh boasted.

"Nah, I'll be more helpful!" Ash said.

"No, I will!"

"No, I will!"

Ash and Goh kept bickering about who would be the best, while Pikachu scampered in circles around their feet.

Just then, Ash's mom came back from her shopping and heard about his plan. "Are you sure you'll be all right, dear?" she asked him. "It'll be a huge commute from here to Pallet Town, you know."

Ash's shoulders slumped. He hadn't thought about the actual details of working in Vermilion City.

"Not a problem," Professor Cerise said. Ash perked up. The professor had a solution! He led the whole group to another part of the building and opened a door to show them a sunny dorm room. Yamper scurried ahead of Ash, Pikachu, and Goh as they went in to check it out. There was a small couch and two desks on one side of the room, and bunk beds and a bookcase on the other. It was perfect!

"We're going to be live-in researchers!" Goh said.

"Awesome! Live-in is the best!" Ash added.

"I call the top bunk!" Goh said as he started to climb up the ladder.

"Hold it!" Ash tugged on Goh to try to pull him down. "I got top-bunk dibs!" Ash tried to start climbing the bunk bed ladder, too, to beat Goh to the top.

"You look like you roll in your sleep, so you're on the bottom!" Goh countered.

"I do not!" Ash said, still trying to get around Goh on the ladder.

"The tallest researcher gets the top bunk!" Goh said, confident that meant him.

"I'm taller than you!" Ash yelled.

"I am!"

"No, *I* am!"

Ash and Goh kept bickering about the top bunk, while Pikachu and Yamper jumped around and played on the bottom bunk.

Ash's mom was watching from the doorway, along with the two professors. "All right, if that's how it's gonna be ... Mimey?" she said, bending down to her Pokémon pal. "Would you mind looking after Ash for me, please?"

Mimey was happy to. "*Mime, mime, mime, mime!*"

Soon, Ash, Goh, and Professor Cerise were saying

good-bye to Professor Oak and Delia as they prepared to drive back to Pallet Town.

"See you later, Mom!" Ash said.

"Oh, before I forget—I want you to eat everything on your plate, even your vegetables!" she replied. "And don't forget to brush your teeth! And also—"

"I know . . . ," Ash said, embarrassed.

"And, Goh?" Delia continued. "Please be a friend to Ash."

"You can count on me," Goh told her.

"Mom, can you please stop?!" Ash cried. His mom was treating him like such a little kid!

Professor Oak said good-bye, too. "I'll be back soon!"

"You're always welcome, Professor Oak," Professor Cerise said. The group staying at the lab waved as Professor Oak started the car and drove off.

"Dad? Ready?" Chloe called to him from up toward the laboratory.

"Oh, sorry! Sorry, can you wait just a bit longer?" he replied. "There's just one final thing I almost forgot about."

What could it be? Ash and Goh were curious.

Back inside the lab, Professor Cerise revealed three Pokémon: Charmander, Bulbasaur, and Squirtle!

"Whoa!" Ash was thrilled to see these familiar first partner Pokémon! But Goh was more uncertain. Professor Cerise explained why the Pokémon were there. "Goh's making his Trainer debut, but I haven't given him a partner Pokémon yet. So, who will it be?" he asked Goh.

"Let's see," Goh said thoughtfully. "I think I'm gonna choose . . . Mew!"

"Huh?" Ash was confused—that wasn't one of the choices! And it was quite an unusual pick for a first partner.

"I've already decided that my very first Pokémon will be Mew!" Goh declared. Ever since he'd seen the amazing, powerful, unique Mew in the forest when he was young, Goh had been dreaming about it. He knew Mew would be the perfect Pokémon partner to show what kind of Trainer he was.

"Wait, you mean the Mythical Pokémon Mew?!" Professor Cerise said in shock.

Goh turned to face Ash, Professor Cerise, and Chloe. He was sure. "It's my future, and I can hold it in the palm of my hand!" he said.

"You're kind of strange, aren't you?!" Ash said in response—meaning it as a compliment!

Goh noticed Ash was sitting on the floor with Charmander in his lap, Squirtle on his back, and Pikachu, Bulbasaur, and Yamper close by. "Not as strange as you, Ash!" Goh said.

"Hey, then I win!" Ash responded, with a cheer.

Goh realized he didn't want to be outdone. "Hold on—I take that back. I'm stranger!"

"No way, I'm way stranger!" Ash replied.

As they kept bickering, Chloe rolled her eyes. "Not that any of this matters . . ."

Professor Cerise chuckled and said, "I'm looking forward to this, and to learning more about Mew!"

Ash and Goh agreed. They couldn't wait to get started as research fellows!

Chapter 8

The next morning in the dorm, Goh's phone alarm clock beeped and beeped. Neither he nor Ash wanted to get up. Goh finally turned the alarm off and said groggily, "Hey, Ash. It's morning already."

"Got it," Ash replied, still half asleep himself. Was he about to oversleep again?

Neither of them moved. Mimey came into their room and cheerily mimed vacuuming the floor—then saw the boys were still asleep, and turned his mime vacuum onto them! It sucked both of their blankets off, making

Ash and Pikachu tumble onto the floor from the bottom bunk.

"*Mime, mime, mime!*" Mimey said, satisfied.

That was one way to get out of bed!

Once Ash and Goh saw what was for breakfast in the lab cafeteria, though, they were happy to be awake. It was an amazing spread!

"Is that all-you-can-eat?" Ash asked, eyeing the many different options.

"What else, Ash?" Goh replied. "Don't forget our special status here—we're this lab's *only* official research fellows!"

Ash noticed another section of the breakfast spread. "Pokémon food, too!"

"*Pika pikaaa!*"

Soon, Ash, Pikachu, Goh, and Mimey were sitting down at a table, digging in (or mime-digging-in!) to their food.

Ash was in the middle of recounting his battle against Lugia the day before when they all heard Yamper yapping. Professor Cerise and Chloe had come

downstairs. They all said good morning and chatted for a few minutes while Ash and Goh ate. Chloe fed Yamper and left for school, and then Professor Cerise turned to go to the lab. "See you later," he said to Ash and Goh.

But the boys didn't want to miss out on anything related to Pokémon research!

"I'll go with you!" Goh said, getting up from the table.

"Me too!" Ash added, cramming a last, giant bite of food in his mouth.

Professor Cerise, Ash, and Goh had just arrived at the main lab when a researcher with blond hair and glasses ran in behind them, panting. He was late to work!

"I'm so sorry!" he said, breathing heavily. "My bus got caught in a huge traffic jam!"

Professor Cerise realized Ash and Goh didn't know the other researchers yet. "I guess I haven't had the chance to formally introduce you all, have I?" he said.

The man who'd gotten in late said, "Hey there, I'm Ren."

"And I have one more assistant," Professor Cerise said. "Her name is–"

"Chrysa," Chrysa said. She was sitting in front of a computer at a cubicle nearby. "It looks like the cause

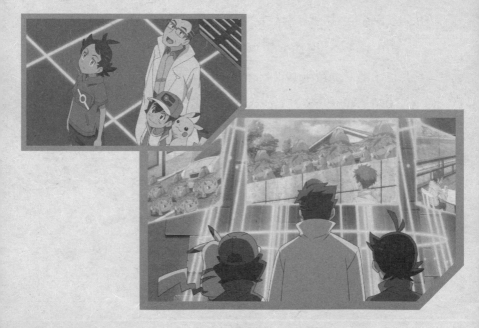

of that traffic jam is already in the news." She pulled up the images on the main computer projection in the center of the lab, and Professor Cerise, Ash, and Goh walked up to it for a closer look.

"Ivysaur!" Ash cried when he saw the screen. There were three pictures, showing a big group of the Grass- and Poison-type Pokémon moving together and blocking traffic in different parts of the city.

"You mean there's been an outbreak of Ivysaur?" Goh asked.

Professor Cerise didn't have a clear answer. "Bulbasaur, Ivysaur, Venusaur . . . They're often first partners to Kanto Trainers, but they still hold a lot of mystery," he said.

"Let's go check it out!" Ash suggested.

Goh agreed. "This will be a great first job as Cerise Laboratory research fellows!" he said.

"You're right!" Ash added. "Ready to rock, Pikachu?"

Pikachu was ready. *"Pika-chuuu!"*

Professor Cerise thought that was a great idea, too. But before they left, he wanted to make sure they had the "most-up-to-date" equipment to do their research. "Ash, do you happen to have your own smart-phone?" he asked. Ash did not, so Professor Cerise pulled one out of his pocket and handed it to him. "Then here you go," he said.

"Thank you so much!" Ash replied.

"Goh, please take yours out, too," Professor Cerise said. Then he pulled out two Poké Balls. He held them up, and with a blast of blue light, a Rotom came out of each!

"Rotom! Wow!" Ash and Goh said together.

"Now take your smartphones and hold them up high," Professor Cerise told them. They both did, and to their surprise, the Rotom disappeared in a bright flash—into their phones!

As they watched, the red phones each sprouted a zigzag antenna, and two bright Rotom eyes and a smile appeared on the back of each.

"Awesome!" Ash and Goh both yelled.

"As you might expect, it's called a Rotom Phone," Professor Cerise explained. "It also serves as a Pokédex."

"Thanks so much!" Ash said. He was very excited

for this new technology—he knew it would come in handy on his next adventure. But there was no time to waste!

He and Goh cheered, "All right, then, let's go!"

Chapter 9

This is weird," Goh said. "I know it should be right around here somewhere . . ." He was looking at his Rotom Phone as he, Ash, and Pikachu walked down a street in Vermilion City, trying to find the Ivysaur traffic jam Ren had told them about.

Then they heard a police whistle blowing in the distance—that must mean the traffic jam was nearby! Goh and Ash ran around the corner and found Officer Jenny in the middle of the road, directing traffic.

"Officer Jenny!" Ash called to her.

"Is there a problem, Officer?" Goh asked.

"Right before your eyes," she replied, and then stepped aside to let a line of Ivysaur cross the road.

Ash and Goh were amazed to see so many of the Seed Pokémon together in person. Goh held up his Rotom Phone, which scanned one of the Ivysaur, identified it, and recited info about it. "A Grass- and Poison-type. The stronger the sunlight it absorbs, the stronger this Pokémon becomes and the larger its flower bud grows."

"So where are all these Ivysaur off to?" Goh wondered aloud. He and Ash watched the line of Pokémon head down the street, but before they could follow, Officer Jenny had some more information for them.

"Oh, while you're here—I'm not sure if this is connected to the Ivysaur, but look," she said. She turned her tablet toward them, which showed a picture of two people and two Pokémon that Ash knew well . . .

"Team Rocket?!" Ash asked, surprised. Were his longtime rivals in Vermilion City? Jessie and James and their Pokémon Meowth and Wobbuffet were almost never up to any good!

Goh had not encountered Team Rocket before. "I read about them on the net," he said. "It said they run around stealing other people's Pokémon . . . But a talking Meowth has got to be a joke, right?"

Ash chuckled. "Yeah, I guess that would be my first thought as well . . . ," he said. He and Pikachu were all too familiar with the talking Meowth!

Officer Jenny continued. "There've been sightings in the immediate area, so we're keeping an eye out," she said. "Please be careful out there."

"Yes, ma'am!" Ash and Goh assured her.

Just then, Pikachu heard something that it wanted to investigate. *"Pika?"* It jumped down from Ash's shoulder and scurried off in the opposite direction from the line of Ivysaur.

Ash and Goh hurried after Pikachu and found themselves in an alleyway. It had a dead end at a brick wall—and there was a lone Ivysaur who kept leaping forward and bashing its head against the wall, over and over again. It looked painful!

"What's going on?" Ash asked.

"It looks to me like it's determined to go forward, but it can't," Goh observed.

Ash wanted to step in. "Let's go give it a hand!" he said.

"No, stop it!" Goh said, grabbing Ash's arm to prevent him from rushing over to the Ivysaur.

"No? Why can't we?" Ash asked.

"We're here to investigate the reason the Ivysaur have suddenly appeared, right?" Goh said. "If you go butting in like that, we're never gonna find out *why*."

Ash was confused—he and Goh clearly had different ideas about how to interact with Pokémon. "What's the harm in helping it out a little?" he said.

"You can't go around trying to fix anything and everything!" Goh replied. "You'll just end up keeping a Pokémon from learning how to help itself!"

"What exactly do you mean by that?" Ash asked.

"If someone's always saving it, it won't learn to live on its own!" Goh explained.

Ash disagreed. "That doesn't make sense!" he

argued. "If something needs help, then I'm gonna help!"

"When a human tries to help a Pokémon in trouble because they feel sorry for it, then that's their emotions talking!" Goh exclaimed. He thought that humans should remain neutral and let Pokémon figure out their problems by themselves.

Ash wasn't convinced. "You call it what you like, but I'm helping it out! Now!" He yanked his arm out of Goh's grip.

Ash approached the Ivysaur slowly. "It's fine!" he said in a friendly voice. "See, I'll help you climb up, okay?"

"*Piii-ka*..." Pikachu wasn't sure it was a good idea.

Ash leaned down to pick up the Ivysaur, saying, "Here goes..." But the Ivysaur was not interested in his help. It gave him an angry look, and then used Tackle on him. It slammed into Ash, throwing him backward onto the street.

"What did you do that for?!" Ash yelled from the ground.

"Told you," said Goh. The Ivysaur wanted to figure its problem out on its own.

Ash was annoyed. "Just leave me alone, would you?" he said to Goh.

"Oh, that's how it is," Goh said, hurt that Ash wouldn't admit he'd been wrong. "And here I thought you were a friend when we rode Lugia. I guess I was way off the mark about that, wasn't I?"

"Look, I don't need you as a friend," Ash said.

"So you're just like everyone else, then, aren't you?" Goh said quietly, disappointed.

Ash stood up. "What did you say?"

"You've done enough," Goh said, taking his Rotom Phone out of his pocket. "I'll investigate this on my own."

"Oh, you will, will you?" Ash replied, annoyed. "Be my guest."

"Don't mind if I do!" Goh said.

"*Piiiikaaa.*" Pikachu did not like seeing Ash and Goh fight.

Suddenly, Ivysaur did something that made them stop arguing and watch. It had realized that slamming into the wall wasn't getting it anywhere. So it used Vine Whip. Its two vines shot upward and wrapped around a light post sticking up above the brick wall from the other side. The vines held tight, and the Ivysaur used them to climb up to the top of the wall!

"Oh, wow!" Ash and Goh were both fascinated to see how Ivysaur had found a solution to its problem. Goh immediately started filming with his phone.

They also both wanted to follow Ivysaur and see where it went next, so they both ran toward the brick wall to climb over it, too. But that didn't mean their argument was over.

"Don't copy me!" Goh said to Ash angrily.

"Right back atcha!" Ash replied.

Ash was more athletic, and he and Pikachu made it to the top of the wall next to the Ivysaur with no problem. They looked at the view from their new vantage point while Goh struggled to climb the last few feet. In the distance, Ash saw a high metal tower that stood far above the surrounding trees. It looked like it was still under construction.

As Goh pulled himself to the top of the wall, dripping with sweat, Ash pulled out his phone. "Rotom, what's that thing?" he asked, holding it up toward the distant tower.

The Rotom Phone answered, "A Pokémon Gym, presently under construction."

Suddenly, Ivysaur used Vine Whip again, attaching its vines to a part of the building on one side of the alley, and leaping forward to a window ledge up ahead. It was on the move!

Ash, Pikachu, and Goh jumped down from the wall to follow it. A nice scent wafted through the air, and Ash and Pikachu tipped their heads back to inhale it.

"Something smells really sweet!" Ash said.

"Let's see," Goh said, thinking hard. He watched Ivysaur walking down the road ahead in the direction of the tower, and realized the scent was coming from the Pokémon. "I get it! It's possible Ivysaur's heading over there to evolve."

"Evolve?" Ash asked.

Goh explained, "When their flower buds give off that sweet smell, it means that they're about to evolve and their flower is going to bloom!"

Ash gasped. That would be so cool to see! He and

Goh looked at each other in excitement. Then they remembered that they were mad at each other and turned away again.

"*Pika-chuuu.*" Pikachu drooped its head.

Chapter 10

Ivysaur kept walking up the tree-lined road. Goh, Ash, and Pikachu kept following it, staying a slight distance apart from one another. Pikachu was the first to notice what was up ahead, at an intersection with another road: more Ivysaur!

"They're gathering in huge numbers over there!" Ash observed. The one Ivysaur they had been following joined a line of Ivysaur marching toward the tower—and there was a line of Bulbasaur next to the line of Ivysaur, too. "They're so cute!" Ash said.

As they watched the Pokémon ahead of them, Goh held up his Rotom Phone toward the tower. "Rotom, any info on this location?"

Rotom showed him a photo taken at the tower's location when construction had just begun. It showed a man and a group of Machop at the building site.

"Oh, Machop worked on it!" Goh said. He loved seeing any info about Pokémon.

Ash heard him and came closer to try to see Goh's Rotom Phone, too, but Goh was reluctant to share.

The Rotom Phone kept giving him information.

"Prior to the construction, this was a sunny field of grass where wild Bulbasaur and Ivysaur, among others, loved to come and soak up the sun," it said.

Soon, they'd followed the group of Pokémon to the base of the tower, where they stopped. One Ivysaur walked forward and studied the tower. "*Saur*."

"*Saur*," all the other Ivysaur and Bulbasaur repeated.

"Ivysaur and Bulbasaur sure look sad," Ash said, solemn.

Goh wasn't sure how Ash knew how the Pokémon felt. "You can tell that?" he asked.

"It's on their faces!" Ash said.

"I don't see anything . . . ," Goh replied, studying the Pokémon in front of them.

Then Goh and Ash both realized that they were having a friendly conversation, but they were supposed to be mad at each other! They turned away from each other with sour expressions.

"*Saur, saur!*" One Ivysaur saw the sun gleaming above the tower and seemed determined to get to it. It used Vine Whip to latch its vines onto one of the platforms on the construction scaffolding around the lower part of the tower. Other Ivysaur and Bulbasaur nearby started doing the same thing, and there was a chorus of vines whipping up and onto the scaffolding as the Pokémon leaped up to the platforms they'd latched on to. Then they used Vine Whip over and over again to reach the next, higher platforms. They were climbing up the outside of the tower.

Goh filmed the Pokémon with his phone. "Maybe they're climbing up because there's more direct sunlight up top?" he guessed.

Ash wasn't spending time thinking about *why* the Ivysaur and Bulbasaur were climbing—he was preparing to climb himself! "Let's go, Pikachu!" he exclaimed. He bounded over to the tower and started climbing up one of the scaffolding poles. Pikachu leaped up easily to the first platform.

Goh was surprised, but he started to see the logic in Ash's action. "So we'll understand if *we* go up?" Then he started trying to climb up the scaffolding, too.

Ash watched a Bulbasaur make its way up to the level above him. "Awesome!"

Then Pikachu drew his attention to what was happening just below their platform. *"Piiika..."* Ash saw that Goh was really struggling to make it up the pole. There was only one thing to do.

"Grab my hand!" Ash said, extending his arm toward Goh. Goh was surprised, but grabbed on gratefully, and Ash helped pull him up to the first scaffolding platform.

"Pika, piiika!" Pikachu cried in delight.

Once they'd caught their breath, Ash looked way up to the top of the tower. "We've gotta get up there!" he said.

Goh bent down on one knee and interlaced his hands to give Ash a step up. "Hop on," he said.

"You sure?" Ash asked.

"Yeah."

"Wow, thanks!" Ash said. He used Goh as a boost to grab on to the pole and the next platform and scrambled up. Then he leaned down and extended his arm. Goh climbed partway up the pole, and Ash helped pull him the rest of the way up. Helping each other made the climbing easier and faster for both of them!

It was a long, long way up. But Ash and Goh worked together to boost, pull, lift, and encourage each other, and at long last, they reached the roof.

"Hey, we made it!" Goh said, pleased and somewhat surprised. He and Ash chuckled and bumped fists in celebration. Pikachu was very happy the boys were friendly again!

Ahead of them were tons of Ivysaur and Bulbasaur, all resting happily with their eyes closed in the sunlight.

"Everybody's getting some sun," Ash observed.

"As the Bulbasaur soak up sunlight, their bulbs will get bigger!" Goh added.

The bulbs on the backs of the Bulbasaur bobbed cheerily, and the flower buds on the backs of the Ivysaur emitted the same lovely scent as before.

"Wow, what a sweet smell!" Ash said.

Goh realized what was going on. "So that's why they came up here in the first place," he said. "They were looking for more direct sunlight."

That inspired Ash. "I know! All you gotta do is act like an Ivysaur to feel what they feel!" he said. Goh was skeptical, but Ash ran over and crouched down in between two Ivysaur. Pikachu hopped onto his back, sitting right where Ash's flower bud would be if he were an Ivysaur. "You really *are* my bud!" Ash said to Pikachu.

"*Piii-kachu.*" Pikachu and Ash both closed their eyes as they happily soaked up the sun.

"It's just like I'm starting to turn into an Ivysaur," Ash said.

Goh doubted whether any person could really feel like they were turning into a Pokémon. But Ash and Pikachu seemed to be having such a good time, he decided to try it out, too. He crouched down on the other side of the Ivysaur from Ash and closed his eyes. "It might be strange, but it *does* feel great!" he said.

The wind blew gently, rustling the trees below and releasing more of the sweet scent from the Ivysaur buds.

"Awesome," both boys said. What a great smell!

"The breeze feels great, too!" Ash said.

"This part of Vermilion City is famous for its amazing breezes," Goh explained. As a local, he knew all about it.

"*Ivy-saur*," the Pokémon between them murmured happily. Suddenly, it started glowing—and so did the other Ivysaur and Bulbasaur all around them!

"Is it evolving?" Goh asked. He and Ash waited breathlessly to see what would happen next.

But what happened was the last thing they expected: A huge net dropped down from the sky and scooped up a ton of Pokémon!

Chapter 11

It was Team Rocket! They were always trying to steal strong and rare Pokémon. Ash could see Jessie, James, Meowth, and Wobbuffet up in their Meowth-shaped hot-air balloon, with the giant net full of Pokémon hanging beneath them. All the Ivysaur and Bulbasaur in the net had immediately stopped glowing.

Goh was surprised. "Team Rocket?! Now this is a first!"

"And it sure won't be the last," Meowth called over the edge of the basket.

Goh shrieked—he was so shocked that Meowth could talk, he couldn't stop taking photos and videos of it with his phone. "It talked! It talked! It really talked!"

"Yeah, yeah . . . get it out of your system," Meowth said.

Ash wasn't surprised. He was ready to get down to business. "Let the Ivysaur and Bulbasaur go, right now!" Ash yelled.

"Ha!" Jessie replied. "How can we resist the pomp and circumstance of a sun-seeking mystery mob?"

"I say, if you can't beat them, steal them!" James added. "Farewell, dear twerp!" They started to fly the balloon away.

"Come back!" Ash commanded.

Goh was still distracted by Team Rocket's manner of speech. "Did he say 'twerp'?" he muttered.

But Ash was determined to protect the Seed Pokémon. "Pikachu, use Iron Tail!" he called.

Pikachu leaped into the air and cut down the net from Team Rocket's balloon with its powerful Iron Tail move. The Bulbasaur and Ivysaur were free again!

Back on the roof, one of the Ivysaur thanked Ash with a grateful *"Ivy-saur."*

"You'll be safe with us now!" Ash replied.

Jessie was outraged. "How dare you take back what was wrongfully ours?!" she called. She turned to Meowth and said, "Get us to ground level."

Meowth brought the balloon down to the roof, and Team Rocket hurried out.

"You don't just cut and run!" Jessie said to Ash, stomping her foot. But before she could act, a Pelipper called out from above, dropping something down to Team Rocket's feet. They each groaned. Their boss had sent them something. It was a strange robot that seemed to be filled with purple Poké Balls.

"So that's our secret weapon?" Meowth asked, skeptical.

"It looks just like a gumball machine," Jessie said.

"Then to make it work, we need a coin," James concluded. Like a gumball machine, it needed a coin put into its slot before it would release the Poké Balls.

"We're fresh out of coin," Meowth said.

Jessie and James looked at the gleaming coin on Meowth's forehead. "No we're not!" they replied—then grabbed Meowth and turned him upside down to stick his head onto the machine.

"That's my Charm!" Meowth cried as he struggled against them, scrabbling his paws against the robot. But Jessie and James turned the knob, and two Poké Balls came out. Meowth sat up, dazed.

"So if this is the Boss's secret weapon, the Pokémon inside are ready to rumble!" Jessie said. She and James each tossed a Poké Ball, crying, "Out we go!"

The Poké Balls flashed open, and info cards dropped into Jessie's and James's hands. They giggled evilly. "It's the Atrocious Pokémon, Gyarados!" Jessie said.

"And the Armor Pokémon, Tyranitar!" James announced.

"That's the Boss for you," Jessie said.

"Leading us to spar along with some feisty Pokémon!" James finished.

Meowth was ready for the battle. "Let's start this show!" he said.

Jessie commanded, "Gyarados, make me proud!"

"Tyranitar, Fire Fang, long and loud!" James cried.

Gyarados and Tyranitar flew forward with menacing roars.

"Pikachu, dodge those!" Ash called.

Pikachu leaped out of the way of the attacks. *"Pikaaa-chu!"*

"Do something epic!" Jessie said to Gyarados. It

used Hydro Pump. A huge stream of water poured out of its mouth.

"Use Dark Pulse!" James said, and Tyranitar immediately began its attack.

"Electroweb, go!" Ash said to Pikachu. All the moves hit each other in midair. "Use Quick Attack!" Ash added, and Pikachu attacked the other two Pokémon before they could use another move. "Awesome!" Ash called in praise.

Goh was impressed. "Sure was!" he said.

Jessie wasn't ready to back down. "One more time!" she said to Gyarados. It used Aqua Tail—which knocked Pikachu backward onto the ground.

Before Pikachu could recover, James told Tyranitar to use Stone Edge. That move also hit Pikachu, flipping it farther backward.

Ash was worried, and so was Goh. "We'd better do something and do it quick!" Goh said.

"I know," Ash said, and ran over to his Pokémon pal. "Pikachu, are you all right?" he asked, his hand on its back. Pikachu made a pained noise, keeping its eyes closed. This wasn't good!

Jessie was ready to take the win. "Let's end this with a double attack!" she said.

"Good choice!" James agreed.

But before they could tell their Pokémon what moves to use, they were surprised by a huge, glowing blast that slammed right into Tyranitar and Gyarados!

"That was Solar Beam!" Ash said in surprise. The Ivysaur had worked together to help Ash and Pikachu out against Team Rocket! Ash thanked them, and Pikachu nuzzled the Ivysaur next to it affectionately.

Jessie and James tended to their Pokémon. Both Pokémon roared to affirm that they were still feeling good.

"I say first we zoom in on those annoying Ivysaur," Jessie began.

"Then scoop up what's left!" James finished.

They called out to their Pokémon, "Hyper Beam, go!" Gyarados and Tyranitar began working together, gearing up for a joint move aimed at the Ivysaur.

But Ash stepped in front of the group of Ivysaur, planting his feet and spreading his arms wide. "Not today . . . ," he said defiantly.

"*Pi-kaaa!*" Pikachu was crackling with electricity and ready to keep battling.

Tyranitar and Gyarados unleashed the double Hyper Beam. At the same time, Ash called out, "Pikachu, use Thunderbolt!"

"*Piiii-kaaaaa-chuuuu!*" An enormous Thunderbolt emerged from Pikachu, clashing with Hyper Beam in midair.

"Let's goooo!" Ash encouraged Pikachu, who used Thunderbolt again . . . and knocked out Gyarados and Tyranitar!

Ash was thrilled with his best Pokémon pal's incredible attack! Even Team Rocket was impressed as they were launched into the air along with their Pokémon.

"That Pikachu's still amazing," Jessie said.

"So, back to plan A!" James agreed.

"To make that Pikachu the catch of the day!" Meowth finished their thought.

"*Wobbuffet!*"

"But first, like old times . . . we're blasting off again!" Jessie cried. And with that, Team Rocket was gone.

Pikachu immediately called Ash's and Goh's attention back to the Ivysaur. They were glowing, just like before. But this time, they weren't interrupted!

"They've all started evolving!" Goh cried. He and Ash were amazed to see this Evolution in action. The Ivysaur bulbs closed all the way . . . and reopened to full flowers once they'd evolved into Venusaur!

"Wow!" What an incredible sight!

Ash held up his Rotom Phone to learn about Venusaur. "A Grass- and Poison-type. It's believed that a nutritious diet and lots of sunlight make Venusaur's flower bloom in more vibrant colors. The flower's scent can calm and heal the human heart," Rotom Phone said.

Ash and Goh watched in fascination as the Venusaur flowers released special, sweet pollen into the breeze. It floated over the Bulbasaur on the tower roof and then spread all across the town, making every plant it touched come into full bloom. The people and Pokémon of Vermilion City were delighted!

Then, one by one, all the Bulbasaur on the roof evolved into Ivysaur!

"Saur! Saur!" The Seed Pokémon on the roof were very happy.

"So the Venusaur came here on purpose to let the wind spread the pollen from their flowers!" Goh observed.

"You're right!" Ash said. "Guess this is what you meant by them learning to live on their own." Even though the field the Pokémon had been planning on visiting now had a tower built on it, they had figured out the perfect spot to soak up the sun and evolve. "Pokémon are just the best!" Ash added.

"For sure!" Goh agreed. "And you know what? Both of you are, too—you're amazing!"

"Huh?" Ash was surprised to hear such praise from Goh.

Goh chuckled. "Nothing, just forget it!"

Back at the Cerise Laboratory, Professor Cerise was fascinated to hear Ash and Goh's account of their day. "Hmm . . . A strange power hidden inside Venusaur's pollen . . . You've done it again, you two!"

Goh smiled proudly. "When it comes to the work of an excellent team like Ash and myself, today is par for the course!"

"Today was such a blast," Ash said happily. "Not only did we get to watch Evolution up close, we got to make friends with a bunch of Ivysaur!"

"First with Lugia, and today, a group of Ivysaur," Professor Cerise said, impressed. "You guys are doing great!"

"Thanks!" Ash replied.

Goh had an idea for Ash. He said shyly, "While you're at it, maybe . . . you could consider being friends with me, too!"

"Wait . . . ," Ash said, confused. "I thought you and I were already friends!"

"Oh, you did?" Goh replied, embarrassed. "That's right, we are!" He and Ash both laughed, pleased to be on such good terms once again.

Suddenly, they were startled by the sounds of an energetic Puppy Pokémon racing by. *"Yamp! Yamp! Yamp!"*

Chloe came through the door. "Hi, I'm home!"

"Welcome back!" her dad said. "You're a little late today . . ."

Chloe sighed. "Every flower in school bloomed all at the same time. I'm in charge of taking care of them, so I'm exhausted!"

Ash and Goh looked at each other and burst out laughing. They knew exactly why that had happened!

"What is with you guys?" Chloe said.

Professor Cerise turned back to business. "With great thanks to our two young and talented research fellows, we learned about the mysteries of Ivysaur," he said. "Thanks a lot!"

"There's still a lot more to do! I can't wait!" Goh exclaimed.

"Yeah! I'm really psyched to learn what our next adventure will be!" Ash added.

The two friends fist-bumped and then ran off to celebrate an amazing day—and many more adventures together ahead!